Face the Music

Adapted by Beth Beechwood

Based on the series created by Michael Poryes and Rich Correll & Barry O'Brien

Part One is based on the episode, "Smells Like Teen Sellout," Written by Heather Wordham

Part Two is based on the episode, "We Are Family—Now Get Me Some Water!,"
Written by Jay J. Demopoulos & Andrew Green

New York

All rights reserved. Published by Disney Press, an imprint of
Disney Book Group. No part of this book may be reproduced
or transmitted in any form or by any means, electronic or
mechanical, including photocopying, recording, or by any
information storage and retrieval system, without written
permission from the publisher. For information address
Disney Press, 114 Fifth Avenue,
New York, New York 10011-5690.

Printed in the United States of America

First Edition
5 7 9 10 8 6 4

Library of Congress Control Number 2007924560
ISBN-13: 978-1-4231-0772-9
ISBN-10: 1-4231-0772-1

For more Disney Press fun, visit www.disneybooks.com
Visit DisneyChannel.com

PART ONE

Chapter One

Miley Stewart, dressed as Hannah Montana and made up to look extra glamorous, was standing on a set and practicing her lines for a commercial she had agreed to do.

She looked deep into the camera. "My time is now . . ." she said in an overly dramatic whisper.

She held up a bottle of perfume. "My perfume is Eau Wow," she added in the same breathy whisper.

"Complete the circle." She pulled the top off the bottle. Right on cue, a group of acrobats wearing red unitards danced over and formed a human circle around her.

"I've never smelled anything like it before," Miley concluded, smiling at the camera.

After a brief pause, she dropped her "perfume character" voice and yelled, "Okay, where's that director? Hannah is ready to smell up the place!"

Lilly Truscott rushed over to her friend. She was dressed as Lola, a member of Hannah's entourage, and was wearing an orange wig. "Let me smell, let me smell," she demanded, grabbing the bottle from Miley. She took a deep, appreciative sniff. "It's light, it's subtle. . . ."

"It's water," Miley told her.

"What a rip-off!" Lilly yelled in disgust.

"Lola, it's just a prop," Miley explained. "The real one will be here any second. It's been completely under wraps. Even *I* haven't smelled it."

"Then how do you know if it's any good?" Lilly asked suspiciously.

"Of course it's good," Miley said. "It's fifty bucks a bottle! And," she added meaningfully, "it completes the circle." Hearing their cue, the acrobats rolled by again.

"Who are those guys?" Lily asked.

"I think they're the circle," Miley said. She practiced her perfume pose, sucking in her cheeks like a model, just as Liza, the commercial's director, walked up.

"Ah, there's my gorgeous little star," she said. Miley turned, thinking Liza was referring to her. But the director blew right on by and walked over to a perfume bottle resting on a pillow. "I'm going to make you look fantastic. This is your moment," Liza said lovingly to the bottle as an armed security guard wheeled it onto the set.

Miley frowned. "What am I, a plate of grits?"

"Here we go again," Liza muttered. She turned and gave Miley an insincere smile. "Hannah, darling, I didn't see you there. When I found out we were going to work together again, all I could say was . . . yee-haw."

"Ah! Liza, you haven't changed a bit," Miley said in a syrupy voice.

"Fantastic," Liza replied with a grin. "That means the eye lift is working." She was nothing if not honest about her ongoing pursuit of perfection through plastic surgery.

At that moment, Miley's dad, Robby Stewart, also dressed in his usual "Hannah's entourage" disguise, walked up. Liza didn't see him, but he could certainly hear her.

"So where's that handsome cowboy daddy of yours?" she asked Miley, adding in a growl, "Liza likey."

Miley saw her dad react in horror. He started to back away, motioning to Miley that she should tell Liza he wasn't there.

"He's in the bathroom," Miley said quickly.

"Oh?" Liza said, her voice filled with hope. After all, if he was *in* the bathroom, eventually he'd have to come *out* of the bathroom—and that would be her moment to pounce!

Miley could see from her father's expression that this wasn't the message he wanted her to convey. She thought fast.

"In Europe," Miley lied.

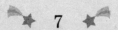

"Oh," Liza said, this time with great disappointment.

"So, what do you say you give me that little bottle of liquid magic and we shoot ourselves a commercial?" Miley asked, trying to change the subject.

"Absolutely," Liza agreed. She turned and called out, "Makeup!"

Miley sat down in the makeup chair and readied herself for her touch-up . . . but the makeup person Liza had summoned wasn't for Miley at all. She went straight over to Liza and touched up her seemingly flawless face.

"Perfect!" Liza exclaimed. "I'm ready."

The shoot began. The camera zoomed in on Hannah's face. "My time is now . . ." she said in a smoky voice.

The camera pulled back to reveal the perfume bottle in the palm of her hand.

"My perfume is Eau Wow," Miley continued. "Complete the circle."

She took the top off the bottle. "I've never smelled anything . . ." She paused to take in the scent. But she nearly choked from the stench and could barely go on. As the acrobats rolled in behind her, getting ready for the big finale, she said with revulsion, "Oh, wow!"

"Cut!" Liza shouted, annoyed. She came out from behind the camera and walked up to Miley, who was waving her hand in front of her nose, trying to get rid of the awful, lingering smell.

"Hannah, darling, a little advertising tidbit," Liza said in her most condescending tone. "When selling a product, gagging and retching—big turnoff."

"Right," Miley said dramatically. "That's why you're the director. One minute."

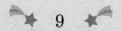 9

She walked over to Lilly, who was still holding the prop bottle in her hand. "Lola, what am I gonna do? This stuff smells horrible."

"Really? I like it. It smells like raspberries," Lilly replied.

"Raspberries, that's it," Miley said, suddenly understanding. "That's what's making me sick."

"What's wrong with raspberries?"

Lilly's innocent question triggered an unpleasant flashback for Miley: she was eight years old and a contestant in the county fair pie-eating contest. She had stuffed herself silly and was elated when the judge announced her as the winner.

"Little Miss Miley Stewart is our new junior pie-eating champion, with five raspberry pies in ten minutes!" he said.

"Yaaaaaay!" little Miley shouted, jumping

up and down on her chair. "I'm a champion, I'm a champion, I'm a champion. I won!"

"And now, to present the award, the governor of Tennessee," the judge said. The governor came forward, beaming. But Miley suddenly was feeling pretty sick to her stomach.

"Uh-oh," Miley said. "I've got a funny, coming out of my tummy. . . ." She groaned, puffed out her cheeks, and opened her eyes wide. Then she proceeded to throw up — all over the governor!

After that day, needless to say, raspberries were no longer appetizing to her.

"That was the last time that governor ever presented that award . . . or wore that suit," Miley concluded. "Now, even a whiff of raspberry makes me sick."

"Hey!" Lilly held up the fake bottle and,

half-kidding, said, "Why don't you just use the fake one? It's only filled with water."

"Lola, you're a genius!" Miley exclaimed.

Lilly smiled. "I am, aren't I?" she said proudly.

Miley marched back to the set, holding the bottle filled with water. She told Liza she was fine; there would be no more retching.

Indeed, everything went great on the second take.

"Complete the circle," Miley said with just the right amount of drama. "I've never smelled anything like it before." Lilly's idea had worked. Miley was really convincing as Hannah Montana, Eau Wow spokesperson.

"And cut!" Liza shouted enthusiastically.

"That was great!" Lilly bubbled. "That was perfect!"

Naturally, Liza assumed that Lilly was

referring to her. "I know," she said smugly. "I've done it again." She turned to address the room. "You and I were brilliant." Liza then took the fake perfume bottle from Miley and walked away.

Lilly turned to Miley. "You're still a plate of grits," she assured her friend.

"It doesn't matter. I'm done with this commercial, and I never have to smell that perfume again." She paused and sniffed. "You're wearing it, aren't you?"

Lilly tried to hide the bottle. "No," she said innocently. Miley gave her a look. Lilly quickly corrected herself. "Yes. I like it," she admitted.

"It doesn't matter. You can't keep it," Miley said, trying to take the bottle from Lilly, who was clutching it tightly.

"I won't wear it around you," Lilly said, tugging the bottle.

"Darn right, you won't," Miley said, pulling harder.

"You're not the boss of me!" Lilly shouted.

"Hey! Let go!" Miley said desperately.

They kept tugging and pulling until finally the bottle spilled all over the place. Well, all over Miley.

Lilly looked at her friend sympathetically. "Oh! You don't look so good."

Miley had turned a little green. She said, "I've got a funny, coming out of my tummy. . . ."

She had the same puffed-out cheeks and wide eyes that had preceded the embarrassing pie-contest incident.

"Everybody clear!" Lilly shouted to the room.

This wasn't going to be pretty.

Chapter Two

Miley spent the rest of the day trying to get rid of the stench of that raspberry perfume. But nothing worked. That afternoon Miley, dressed in a robe, shower cap, and goggles, dunked her head in a giant bowl of tomato juice. Lily sat nearby reading a magazine. The kitchen timer was ticking away.

"Miley," Lilly piped up. "It's been a half hour. If that tomato juice was going to get rid of the smell, it would've worked by now."

"You're right," Miley admitted, lifting her head from the bowl. "This is getting ridiculous."

"Getting?" Lilly raised her eyebrows and looked at her friend skeptically. "You passed ridiculous when you took a bath in tuna fish."

"Hey, it said it worked on some stink Web site." Miley pulled off her goggles. "I should've backed out of the commercial the minute I smelled that perfume. Now I smell worse than Uncle Earl after he was drilling for oil and hit the sewage pipe."

"Okay," Lilly said. "If I haven't said this before: I don't ever want to meet Uncle Earl."

Mr. Stewart walked in just in time to overhear Lilly's comment. "Uncle Earl's not that bad," he said. "The one you don't want to meet is Aunt Max. Talk about your bearded lady." He handed Miley a bag. "Anyhow, honey, I found this old bag of kitty litter out in the garage. It's supposed to activate when you scratch it. Might be worth a shot."

He and Lilly shared a big laugh at the notion, but Miley wasn't amused.

"Dad, it isn't funny," Miley whined. "You didn't see what I went through."

"I'm sorry, honey, I was a little busy," Mr. Stewart said kindly.

"Yeah," Miley said sarcastically. "Hiding from liposuction Liza." She walked over to the sink to wash the gunk off her face.

"I wasn't hiding," he said, trying to defend himself. He turned to Lilly, figuring she would appreciate his sense of humor about all this. "I just got stuck trying to get out the bathroom window. I'm sorry, that lady is just plain weird."

He and Lilly were still chuckling about his narrow escape when Miley's brother, Jackson, came leaping down the stairs, wearing a camouflage outfit complete with headband and face paint.

"Hi-ya!" Jackson said cheerfully to the group.

"She's not the only one . . ." Lilly sang to herself. She couldn't help it. If Mr. Stewart could call Liza weird . . .

"Dad, I'm about to make you proud," Jackson said.

"You're going to go back upstairs and change?" Mr. Stewart asked hopefully.

"No, I'm going to make an audition tape. You are looking at the next million-dollar winner of . . . *Teen Wilderness Challenge.*"

Lilly jumped up when she heard this. "I

love that show!" she shouted. "Last night the girl from Pittsburgh had to eat a live millipede!" She said this as if it were a good thing.

"Yeah, poor kid," Mr. Stewart said. "She had nine hundred legs down before that little critter hung a left and went out her nostril."

"Jackson, you wouldn't last one day on *Teen Wilderness Challenge*," Miley said as she finished toweling off her face.

As if on cue, a fly buzzed into the room.

"Oh, yeah?" Jackson replied to Miley. "Check it out." He struck a tai chi pose and closed his eyes dramatically. Then he opened them, snatched the fly out of the air, and popped the poor thing in his mouth! They all stared at him in astonishment — until he started coughing. The fly flew back out of his mouth completely unharmed and still buzzing.

"I throw the little ones back," Jackson said offhandedly, trying to keep his macho persona intact. "It's the way of the hunter."

And then the hunter was off, out the front door and headed to . . . well, to the beach.

Jackson was meeting Miley's friend Oliver Oken at the beach to film his audition video for *Teen Wilderness Challenge*. When he got there, he found Oliver ready and waiting, video camera in hand. Jackson told Oliver his plan for the video, and they got started right away.

"My name is Jackson Rod Stewart, and I'm your next Teen Wilderness champion," Jackson said into the camera. "You get a lot of audition tapes of people telling you what they're going to do. Well, I'm going to *show* you." He struck a martial arts pose and shouted, "Hi-yah!"

"I'm going to survive for the next two weeks on this beach. My only tools: these," he said, displaying his hands. "And this." He pointed to his head. "And a whole lotta this," he added, pounding on his chest. "And of course, these." He pointed to his ears. "And these." He pointed to his eyes. "But that doesn't really count—I always use those. Anyway, I'll be completely isolated from all of civilization."

Just then, a Frisbee came out of nowhere and hit Jackson right in the chest. Oliver turned off the camera as a little boy and his mother came running over. The boy grabbed his Frisbee, muttering, "Sorry."

The boy's mother looked at Jackson in his survival gear and said nervously to her son, "Oh, honey, get away from the strange man."

They walked away quickly. But Jackson didn't care if they thought he was strange. He only cared about getting on the show.

"You can edit that out, right?" he asked Oliver.

"Sure," Oliver replied, but he looked concerned. "But I don't get it. You didn't bring any food. How are you going to survive out here?"

"Off the land, man!" Jackson said with enthusiasm. "Nature's bounty is abundant. Now shoot this. I'm gonna go up that tree and get some coconuts for dinner."

Oliver switched the camera on as Jackson started to climb.

"Get in tight on my bear tooth," Jackson directed, referring to his necklace. "It lets them know I'm a 'war' hero." He climbed out of the camera's view. A minute later, he shouted down to Oliver, "Hey, double O, I got two of them!"

The next second, Jackson came tumbling out of the tree, coconuts and all.

Oliver ran over to where his friend lay sprawled on the ground. "Are you okay?"

Jackson gasped between breaths, "Landed right on . . . the coconuts."

Miley was right, he thought. This survival stuff *is* harder than it looks on TV.

Chapter Three

Back at the Stewart household, Miley found her father out on the deck, looking through binoculars. "Dad, I need to talk to you about something," she said.

"Hang on, bud," Mr. Stewart replied, his eyes glued to the binoculars. "I'm watching your brother. He's been trying to open up a coconut for over half an hour." He watched as Jackson, still at the beach with Oliver, hurled a coconut against a rock. But instead of cracking open, the coconut bounced right back at Jackson and knocked him to the ground.

Mr. Stewart couldn't hear this, but Jackson looked at Oliver and said, "Oliver . . ."

"I know," Oliver said. "Edit it out."

Laughing, Robby finally lowered the binoculars. "I don't know why I pay for cable when I have a son like him." Then he saw the look on his daughter's face and quickly got serious. "So, what's on your mind, bud?"

"Daddy, is there any way you can call the Eau Wow people and have them stop that commercial from going on the air?"

"This thing's really eating at you, isn't it?" Mr. Stewart said.

"Yeah, that perfume makes me sick," Miley said. "How can I tell the world I love it?"

Mr. Stewart nodded supportively. "If that's the way you feel, I'll call the company and we'll put a stop to it right now."

"Thanks, Dad. That's a load off." Miley felt lucky to have him as her manager right then. She gave him a big, grateful hug to let him know how much he meant to her.

Her dad pulled away and said, "Now, cheer yourself up. Take a look at your brother." He handed Miley the binoculars, which she took eagerly. She loved watching Jackson make a fool of himself.

"Ooh! Whoa!" she said, wincing at what she saw through the binoculars. "That's gotta hurt!" She smiled at her father. "But you're right, it did cheer me up . . ."

As they headed into the house, the doorbell rang.

". . . and so does knowing that Hannah Montana isn't gonna lie to the whole world," Miley added.

Mr. Stewart opened to door to find a

delivery man standing before him.

"Delivery from Eau Wow perfume," the man said.

"I hope it's muffins," Mr. Stewart said excitedly.

Miley looked at him as though he were nuts. "I love when they send those teeny tiny muffins with little chocolate chips in them, and icing on the top," he explained.

Miley rolled her eyes. "Dad, just bring it in."

The delivery man looked skeptical. "Uh, yeah," he said. "I don't think it'll fit through the door."

Mr. Stewart seemed a little disappointed. Under his breath, he said, "I was hoping for muffins." But when he and Miley headed out the front door, they found themselves staring at something that left them both nearly speechless.

"Oh . . ." Mr. Stewart couldn't even finish his thought.

"Wow." Miley did it for him.

They were looking at a brand-new red Mustang convertible, wrapped with a giant bow. The top was down, revealing a gleaming interior. The pink license plate read, "Eau Wow." And there was a card propped on the windshield.

Mr. Stewart snapped out of his stupor, picked up the card, and read it out loud. "'You wowed us. Hope this wows you. Your Eau Wow family.'"

"Daddy," Miley squealed. "It's beautiful!

"Yep," Mr. Stewart agreed. "Too bad we gotta send it back."

"Say what?" Miley said. She almost got whiplash from snapping her head away from the shiny car to stare at her dad.

"Hey, Mile, they're not going to let us

keep it once you back out of that commercial," he explained.

"The only thing I'm backing out of is this driveway in my sweet new ride," Miley said.

"Now hold your horses. I thought you said you couldn't stand the smell of that perfume," Mr. Stewart reminded her.

"Right," Miley admitted. "Now all I'm smelling is new car. . . ." Then she spotted the cherry on top. She picked up a basket from the front seat. ". . . and muffins!"

"Eeee doggies!" Mr. Stewart hooted. "Ooh! Those chocolate-chip ones."

The next morning, Miley and Lilly were enjoying Miley's new car . . . in the Stewart's driveway. Miley sat behind the steering wheel, music blaring from the radio and her hair blowing in the wind. The wind actually came from a fan that Lilly was holding, but it helped create the illusion that they were really driving.

"Man, this car handles like a dream. She really hugs the road," Miley said.

"Just think," Lilly said. "One day you'll have your permit, and then you can really drive this thing."

Miley was positively giddy at the thought. "I know," she giggled.

"Selling out was the best thing you ever did," Lilly assured her friend.

"I didn't sell out," Miley said defensively.

"Oh, please," Lilly said, rolling her eyes. "You did a commercial saying you loved something that makes you want to yack."

"Okay, maybe a little," Miley admitted. "But everybody exaggerates in commercials. I mean, do you really think that football player's mom follows him around with a can of soup? Doubt it!" She was trying to make herself feel better. But, in fact, she wasn't completely comfortable with the decision she had made.

Her father came outside just then, almost as if her conscience had decided to make a personal appearance. "Hey, Mile," he said, "the Eau Wow people called. You still sure about going through with this?"

She ignored her gut and beeped the horn. "That's car talk for 'oh, yeah, baby!'" Miley said with a smile.

"Okay, then congratulations. Tomorrow night you're going to be talking about how much you love Eau Wow on *The Real Deal with Collin Lasseter.*"

Miley got out of the car and walked over to her father. Lilly quickly took the opportunity to slide into the driver's seat. "Collin Lasseter?" Miley said nervously.

"That's the biggest interview show on TV."

"Yup, I know, bud." Mr. Stewart gave his daughter a thoughtful look. "There's still time to pull the plug on this."

"And give back our car?" Lilly shouted in disbelief. Miley shot her a look. Lilly went on more calmly, "I mean, you do what you feel is right. I'm just going to sit here and enjoy what time I have left with . . . Maria." Her voice trembled with emotion. Apparently, she had named the car.

"Don't worry, Lilly. Our car is not going anywhere," Miley said. She turned back to her father. "You tell Collin I'll be there."

"Okay, then I'll go make the call." As Mr. Stewart headed back inside, Lilly hopped out of the car. She jumped up and down, hugging Miley.

"I'm so proud of you. I could never go in front of the whole world and lie. When I tell my dad I've finished my homework when I haven't, I start giggling like an idiot," Lilly said.

"Well, that's the difference between me and you," Miley said confidently. "I can go on Collin Lasseter and say I love Eau Wow." But she giggled as she finished her sentence.

"What was that?" Lilly asked.

"Nothing," Miley shrugged, hoping it really *was* nothing. "I just thought of something funny, that's all. It's not like I was laughing because I was lying."

But, as she laughed again, she looked accusingly at Lilly. "You did this to me."

As night fell, Jackson and Oliver were trying to stay committed to their project. Oliver held the camera steady while Jackson, scruffy and tired from his long day foraging for food, held a very small crab up to the camera lens. Behind him were his sleeping bag and beach umbrella, or what Jackson described as his "tent."

"After a six-hour hunt, I finally bagged this beauty," Jackson said breathlessly. "My first solid food in six hours and two minutes. And now, I will start my own fire and cook my feast."

He put the crab down and got to the task of making a fire. Furiously, he rubbed two sticks together, not noticing when the crab began to crawl away. "Though you gave me a fierce battle, oh mighty crab, in the end your primitive little brain was no match for mine."

Jackson glanced up, only to discover that his foe had in fact won. The crab was gone.

"Oh, man! Where'd he go?" Jackson whined. "Dang flabbit! Oliver?"

"Don't worry," Oliver reassured him for the millionth time that day. "It's erased. But I think you should know at this point we only have twenty-seven seconds of usable footage."

"Who cares about footage? I'm starving." Jackson's enthusiasm for surviving in the wild and appearing on TV had apparently waned quite a bit over the last six hours.

"Tell me about it. Remember, we're going through this together. You and me, side by side, living on nothing but—" Oliver's pep talk was interrupted when a man holding a cardboard box arrived on the beach.

"Pizza delivery for Oliver Oken," the guy said.

"Right here, dude," Oliver said, handing over some money and taking the pizza.

Jackson was ecstatic. Food had arrived!

His struggle was over! "Oliver, you're brilliant," he said to his cameraman. "Hey, give me a slice."

"I can't do that, man," Oliver said.

"C'mon," Jackson begged. He reached into his pocket. "I'll give you . . . three pukka shells and these magic fire sticks."

Oliver tried to get back into his pep talk. "Jackson, get a grip. You're stronger than this. Sure, I could give you this pizza," he said, opening up the box, ". . . and you could stuff yourself with the pepperoni and the sausage and the cheesy filled crust. But you don't want that."

Jackson was practically drooling. "I don't?"

"No!" Oliver shouted. "You're a Teen Wilderness champion. You've got this," he said, pointing to his head, "and this," he pointed to his heart, trying to remind Jackson of his speech earlier. "And all that other stuff. I wish I could be like you," he said, taking a big bite of his pizza slice. "But I'm weak. That's why I'm going to eat this in my tent." He disappeared into his tent—which was starting to look to Jackson more like a deluxe hotel suite—and zipped up the flap, leaving Jackson all alone and utterly . . . pizza-less.

"Fine, you go ahead," Jackson said in a huff. "I don't need your stinkin' pizza." He scraped some green stuff off a rock, shouting, "I've got rock grass! And seaweed and fresh air and nature's very own moonlight!"

Jackson could hear the sound of a television clicking on inside Oliver's tent. He listened—desperately wanting to get back to civilization—and heard a newscaster say, "Coming up on Channel 24 weather, freak thunderstorms along the coast! We might even see some hail!"

Jackson quickly returned to the task of building a fire. Thunder rumbled overhead as he frantically rubbed his sticks together and said to no one in particular, "I can do this. I can do this. I'm a Teen Wilderness champion, I am a Teen Wilderness champion. Ooh! Got a splinter." He stopped to look at his finger. "Blood! The blood of a warrior." As the rain started to pour down, Jackson realized that he had a very long night ahead of him.

Meanwhile, Mr. Stewart was at home in the kitchen, watching the rain pound against the windows.

"Man, that rain is really coming down out there. I hope Jackson's okay," he said as he threw a steak into a pan on the stove.

With his back turned, Mr. Stewart didn't see his son's face in the window, illuminated by a flash of lightning. Jackson looked like a wild man—dripping wet, face paint smeared down his cheeks, and his clothes tattered from his day "in the wild."

When Mr. Stewart turned to get something out of a cabinet, Jackson, hunched over like a caveman, slipped inside and crouched behind the kitchen island.

Mr. Stewart seasoned his steak, then turned to put the seasoning back in the cabinet.

Jackson saw his chance. He popped up, speared the steak with a stick he had whittled, and darted out of the room, silently laughing at his victory.

Mr. Stewart turned back around to find his steak missing. "What in tarnation—" He looked around, trying to figure out where his steak had gone. Meanwhile, Jackson had sneaked back outside, pausing to gloat at his father through the window. But Mr. Stewart had missed the whole thing, leaving him wondering what in tarnation had happened to his steak!

Chapter Four

By the next day, it had stopped raining. Miley had a big day as Hannah ahead of her. She and her entourage—her dad and Lilly in disguise—had arrived on the set of *The Real Deal*. Miley was getting some last-minute makeup applied before her big interview.

"Thanks," she said to the makeup artist. "That's good." She was trying to be cheerful, but she couldn't get over the fact that she was lying . . . just to get a car. Lilly must have sensed her friend's unease, because she came over to reassure her.

"Hannah, I just want you to remember this: whatever happens out here, I love you . . . and I really love that car. Please don't blow this."

Okay, so maybe "reassure" wasn't the right word exactly.

"Lola," Miley said to Lilly, "chillax. I got it all figured out. All I have to do is not lie. If I don't lie, then I won't giggle. For example, ask me what I think of the perfume."

"What do you think of the perfume?" Lilly asked.

"It's like nothing I've ever smelled before," Miley said, and paused. "You see? No giggles."

Mr. Stewart walked over to the girls with a distressed look on his face.

"Darlin', the more I think about it, the more I think going on this show's a bad idea," he admitted to his daughter.

"Oh, Daddy, you worry too much," Miley said.

"What if he brings out a bottle of that perfume and you get a whiff of it?" Mr. Stewart asked.

"Thought of that," Miley said proudly. "I got about a pound of vapor rub in my nose. Right now I could smell one of Jackson's dirty socks and live to tell the tale."

Her father nodded appreciatively. "I'll have to remember that next time I visit Uncle Earl and he's cooked up a pot of that three-bean chili." He looked at Miley more seriously. "You're sure you're okay?"

"Trust me, Dad, everything is going to be fine." Miley thought she was golden, but then she let out a big laugh.

"What's so funny?" Mr. Stewart asked.

Miley tried to cover up her newly discovered nervous habit. "What's *not* funny, Dad? You've got to learn to laugh more. It's gonna be a breeze." She giggled again.

Lilly piped up then. "Liza alert," she warned.

They all looked up to see Liza, dressed as a cowgirl, approaching them.

She was smiling and waving. "Howdy, partner!" she bellowed.

Mr. Stewart yelped, "Ahh!" and hurried away from the group. Liza came over anyway, saying to Miley, "Just came by to wish you luck." Then she turned her attention back to Miley's dad. "Wait up, cowboy!" she called in Mr. Stewart's direction.

Miley glared at Lilly. "You had to plant that giggling thing in my head."

"Well, look on the bright side," Lilly said. "You can always cover giggling by saying something was funny. It's not like you're Oliver. I mean, when he lies, he hiccups."

Moments later, Miley was seated next to Collin Lasseter himself. This was it, no backing out now. As the show came back from a commercial break, Collin said to the audience, "And we're back with pop sensation Hannah Montana." He looked at Miley. "We've talked about your new CD and your European tour. Let's get the real deal on this commercial. Is it true? Had you really never smelled anything like it before?"

Miley took a deep breath and said, "I can honestly say, throughout all the perfumes that I've worn, it is totally unique, and that's the truth." She paused, waiting for the giggling to commence, but it didn't. She was elated.

"So you weren't just acting," Collin prodded, "you honestly love this stuff?"

This was tricky. Miley searched for a way to answer. "Uh, well, have you seen the bottle? It's beautiful. Round with a little point."

He wasn't going to let her get away with that, Miley knew. "Yeah, it's great. But I was asking about what's inside. Do you like the perfume, yes or no?" Collin pressed.

"Well, of course the answer has to be . . ." Miley crossed her fingers before she said, ". . . yes."

And then she giggled.

"Well, that's good to hear. I'm glad you're not one of those celebrities who goes out and pushes something she doesn't believe in," Collin said.

Miley couldn't believe how hard this was. But she kept on. "That's not me." Another giggle. She tried to cover by taking a sip of water.

"What an adorable laugh you have," Collin said with a smile.

"Glad you like it," Miley said nervously. "You're gonna be hearing it quite a lot."

"Great," Collin said. "Artie says our switchboard is going crazy. So let's take some calls."

Miley wasn't sure how much longer she could keep pretending she liked this perfume, but she knew the call-ins were the most important part of the show. So, a little reluctantly, she said, "Okay."

Collin punched a button on the switchboard and said, "Caitlin from Michigan, you're on with Hannah Montana."

"Hannah," Caitlin from Michigan said

giddily, "I love you, and I can't wait to smell like you! Do you wear Eau Wow every day?"

"Well . . . not every day," Miley admitted.

"Why not?" Collin asked.

"I don't want to waste it," Miley said. This time, she giggled *and* hiccupped.

Lilly! she thought, as she covered her mouth. Again, she had to cover. "There was an ant," she told Collin, brushing an imaginary ant off the desk.

"You okay?" Collin asked his guest.

"Yeah, I'm just a little nervous being on your show." Miley had to think fast. "You're actually much more handsome in person," she said confidently. Only she hiccupped again, and then she giggled. She struggled to cover her mouth, trying to hide all of the awful sounds coming out of it.

"Isn't she the cutest thing?" Collin

gushed. "Big star like her still gets nervous. You know, when I get nervous, I sweat like a pig." He laughed.

"Thanks, Collin," she said, trying to smile. This was just a little too much information for Miley. "Good to know."

"Let's take our next caller." Collin pressed another button. "Brianna from Georgia."

"Hannah, I'm such a big fan," Brianna gushed over the phone. "I can't believe I'm talking to you. I hear your perfume smells like raspberries. I love raspberries. Don't you love raspberries?"

Is this a sick joke? Miley wondered. "Well . . . I really don't like singling out any one fruit as my favorite . . . so unfair to the other fruits." She was trying her best, but now beads of sweat were forming on her forehead. She wasn't sure how much longer she could keep this up.

"But it's in your perfume, so you've got to like raspberries, right?" Collin asked, thinking this was an innocent question. "Yes or no?"

"Uh . . . yes. I mean, who doesn't like a good raspberry?" This was the only answer Miley could muster. By now, the beads of sweat had turned into a steady stream. "Thanks for the call, Brianna," Miley continued. "Read a book, eat your vegetables, always be polite."

"Thanks, Hannah. I love —" Before poor Brianna could finish, Miley reached over and disconnected the call.

"So, Collin, how about that hailstorm last night?" she asked, wiping the sweat off her forehead and inadvertently flinging some of it right at the show's host.

"Hannah, you need a tissue or a . . . bath towel?" Collin joked.

Miley, who now looked as if she had just run under a sprinkler, replied casually, "No thanks. I'm good." That answer might have been a mistake, because she giggled and hiccupped again. She tried to gather herself by taking a deep breath, but she got a mouthful of sweat instead.

Lying clearly wasn't for her.

Chapter Five

Miley and Lilly stood in the driveway, preparing for the sad moment.

"How ya feelin', bud?" Mr. Stewart came outside and put his arm around Miley.

"I'm really glad I told the Eau Wow people that I couldn't endorse their perfume. The truth is always the best thing. Even though sometimes it hurts. It really, really hurts."

Miley watched sadly as her precious car

was driven out of the driveway. Lilly, dressed all in black, including a black veil, dabbed at her eyes with a tissue.

"I'm going to miss her so much. I'll never forget you, Maria," Lilly said wistfully. Miley put her arm around her friend to console her, and they headed back toward the house.

"Lilly, calm down," Miley said. "It's really not that great of a car anyway." But she giggled and hiccupped as she said it. She could never lie again. "I'm going to miss you, too, Maria," she said to the departing car.

"It's okay. We'll survive," Lilly assured her dramatically.

"Hey, speaking of surviving," Mr. Stewart said. "Have you heard from your brother? I just got a call from that *Teen Wilderness Challenge* show. He's been turned down."

"How do you think he's going to take it?" Lilly asked.

Just then, Jackson, still sporting his tattered camouflage outfit, came swinging across the driveway on a vine, yelling like Tarzan. He swiped the banana Mr. Stewart had been eating and swung right back to wherever he had come from.

Miley looked at Lilly. "Not so good."

PART TWO

Chapter One

It was a typical day in the Stewart household. As usual, Miley had a big event to rehearse for—the American Teen Music Awards. And, as usual, Jackson was preventing her from doing so by being . . . well, Jackson.

Miley sat at the piano in the family room. She played a few notes, then sang the song's opening lines.

She was interrupted by sirens blaring

from the television. Jackson was playing his favorite video racing game. It was incredibly loud and annoying.

"You'll never take me alive, coppers!" Jackson shouted to the video-game cops.

Miley rolled her eyes at her brother and tried to return to her song.

She sang another few lines, attempting to ignore Jackson. The screeching and honking from his game interrupted her yet again, as did his ranting.

"Outta the way, grandma! I've got the po-po on my tail!" Jackson yelled.

Miley had had enough of this. There was no way she could get anything done with Jackson around.

"Jackson, I'm trying to rehearse for the American Teen Music Awards."

"Yeah, yeah, don't worry. You're not bothering me," Jackson said, oblivious.

Miley decided to get to the point. "But *you're* bothering *me*."

"Ohhhh, right," her brother said, feigning concern. "Don't care." He shrugged and turned his attention back to the game. "Look out, cow!" There was another sound of a car screeching, followed by a loud crash. The poor virtual cow let out a mournful "moo."

"Ooooh, look at that heifer fly . . . right into the marching band!" Jackson said gleefully.

"Hey, Jackson, you know, you have a *real* car," Miley said, hoping he'd take the hint. Then she added, "Here's a thought — get in it and drive away."

"I would if I had real gas, which costs real money, which Rico doesn't pay me a real lot of," Jackson said, referring to his job at Rico's Surf Shop snack bar.

"So ask Rico for a raise," Miley said.

Jackson put on his best country bumpkin voice. "Ask for a raise," he said. "Gee, that sounds like a good idea. Oh, wait," he said, returning to his normal voice. "I did. It's not gonna happen. Rico's vicious, ruthless, and completely inflexible."

Miley decided that if she ever wanted the house to herself, she would have to get Jackson a raise so he could make himself scarce from time to time. That afternoon, she dragged Lilly over to Rico's Surf Shop. She wanted help convincing Jackson's boss that he should pay her brother more money.

When they got there, they found Rico practicing a tango, using a broom as his dance partner. The two girls watched as Rico dipped the broomstick gracefully and ended the routine with a flourish.

Miley remembered Jackson's comment

about Rico. "He looks pretty flexible to me," she remarked.

"To me, he looks like a very lonely munchkin," Lilly joked.

"Well, Jackson can't leave the house until that munchkin gives him a raise," Miley said, reminding Lilly of their mission. "Then maybe finally I can get some rehearsing done. Wish me luck."

"Just remember," Lilly said, putting on a munchkin voice from *The Wizard of Oz*, "follow the yellow brick road."

Miley walked up to Rico, who was still dancing with the broom.

"Hey, Rico, that is one lucky broom," Miley said, pretending to swoon.

"Can it, toots," Rico said shortly. "I'm working on my tango."

"Have you gotten taller?" Miley asked, amping up the flattery.

But Rico was on to her. "Your brother's not getting a raise," he said.

"I wasn't going to say that," Miley insisted. But she saw Rico's disbelieving look and reconsidered her approach. "Okay, fine, I was. But—"

"All right, I'll make you a deal, Twiggy," Rico offered. "I'll ask my dad to give him a raise, if you be my partner for a ballroom dance competition."

Miley laughed at the thought. "Ballroom dancing?"

"Laugh all you want. Chicks dig it. And I dig chicks," Rico said smoothly. "So, what do you say? You wash my back, I wash your brother's."

"Okay, first, ewwww," Miley said. "Second, I think it's *scratch* my back. And third, ewwww."

"Fine," Rico said firmly. "No dance partner, no raise."

Part One

"Of course it's good," Miley said. "It's fifty bucks a bottle!"

"I found this old bag of kitty litter out in the garage. It's supposed to activate when you scratch it. Might be worth a shot," said Mr. Stewart.

"My name is Jackson Rod Stewart, and I'm your next *Teen Wilderness* champion," Jackson said into the camera.

"That's gotta hurt," said Miley. "But you're right, it did cheer me up."

"I thought you said you couldn't stand the smell of that perfume," Mr. Stewart reminded Miley.

"Just think," Lilly said, "one day you'll have your permit and you can really drive this thing."

"All I have to do is not lie," Miley told Lilly. "If I don't lie, then I won't giggle."

"Lilly, calm down," Miley said. "It's really not that great of a car anyway."

"Jackson, I'm trying to rehearse for the American Teen Music Awards," Miley said.

"Here you go," Oliver said. "Two fresh waters for m'ladies."

"I was just trying to help," Miley explained. "And besides, Jackson, I said I was sorry."

"You're being a very good sister," Lilly said. "And who knows, maybe he'll rise to the occasion."

"You have something in your teeth,"
Lilly whispered.

"Here you are, ladies," said Oliver. "My newest
concoction . . . the Smokin' Oken Smoothie."

"I'm just gonna say, 'Jackson, you're—'" Miley was interrupted. "—carrying a balloon-heart bouquet," she finished.

"I've got a special job for you," Miley said. "And it's the only thing I need you to do today. . . . Everything else, once again, stay away."

"Okay, fine, then no more smiley Miley," she snapped. She grabbed Rico by the lapels and lifted him off the ground. "Listen here, bub, my brother's sick of being pushed around, and he ain't gonna work here anymore unless you give him a raise."

"Okay, okay, you win," Rico conceded.

"I do?" she said, surprised.

"Yeah," Rico said. "He's fired."

"Really?" Miley asked, even more surprised. This *so* wasn't part of the plan!

Chapter Two

Miley went home to figure out how to fix the mess she had just made. She gulped when she found Jackson already dressed for work. She knew she had to break the news to him, and it wasn't going to be easy.

"Hey, Jackson, where you going?" Miley asked her brother, stalling for time.

"Well, I was heading to Jessica Alba's for movies and kettle corn, but then I decided I'd rather spend six hours making minimum wage at Rico's," Jackson said sarcastically.

"Whoa, whoa, whoa, you know what, I've been thinking," Miley said quickly. "And you're right, that little runt doesn't pay you enough. In fact, I think you should quit." She smiled at him, her heart full of hope. Maybe this strategy would work! Maybe Jackson would turn in his resignation! Maybe she would never have to tell him how badly she had screwed up. . . .

"I'm not gonna quit," Jackson said.

Darn, Miley thought.

"You're right! He isn't worth your time or trouble," Miley said brightly. "I'll do it for you." She started to walk away.

"Mile—" Jackson tried to stop her.

"Don't need to thank me, brother. That's why we're here," she said, and tried to leave again.

Jackson looked at Miley suspiciously. "Miles? What did you do?"

Miley hesitated, but she knew she couldn't dodge the truth any longer.

"See, I maayyy have asked Rico to give you a raise, and it maayyy have not gone as well as I'd hoped," Miley explained.

"Oh, great, what'd the little weasel do? Cut back my hours?" Jackson asked.

Hmm, Miley thought. That *was* what had happened—kind of.

"Just a tad," she said.

When he heard that, Jackson angrily took off for the snack bar with Miley right behind him. She knew her brother was going to need some support.

"Don't worry, Jackson, as soon as Rico sees how dead the place is without you, he'll beg for you to come back," Miley said.

But as they approached Rico's, they

could hear music playing and, as they got closer, they saw that the place was hopping. "Or not," she finished.

"What's happened? How did it get so busy?" Jackson asked.

"Simple," Rico said as he danced over to them. "I brought in a professional."

The crowd parted to reveal the back of Rico's new employee, a dark-haired young man performing for the customers. First, he juggled two bottles of water behind his back. Then, as he flipped them into the air, he spun around to face Jackson and Miley. They looked at him in shock.

The professional was Oliver!

He caught the bottles smoothly and poured water into two cups that were sitting on the counter.

"Here you go," Oliver said to two pretty girls standing in front of him. "Two fresh waters for . . . m'ladies." He pointed and winked at the girls.

"I gotta tell you, getting rid of this piece of seaweed—" Rico pointed at Jackson. "—was the best thing I ever did."

In response, Jackson picked Rico up off the ground the very same way Miley had earlier that day.

"Look, Rico, I want my job back," Jackson demanded.

"Again with the lifting!" Rico screeched.

Jackson put Rico down, realizing that the physical approach, while satisfying, probably wasn't helping matters.

"I'm sorry," he said. "This wasn't my fault."

Miley picked up on his cue. "He's right," she volunteered. "It was mine, and there's got to be something I can do. Hey, do you still need a dance partner?"

"Too late, angel face," Rico said as he snapped his fingers, causing a statuesque dancer to spin into his arms. "This is Carmen," he told them. "She's from Arrrrgentina, the land of the tango."

The two of them danced off, leaving Miley and Jackson by themselves.

"Great," Jackson said to Miley. "Thanks to you, I'm from 'flat brrrrroke.'" He rolled his r's to imitate Rico. "The land of unemployment."

When they got home, Miley and Jackson found their father planted on the couch in the same spot Jackson had been in earlier, playing the video game that had started the whole mess.

"Yee-haw! Oh, yeah," Mr. Stewart hooted. "Man, this jalopy races faster than Uncle Earl's heart at a Shakira concert!"

Jackson stomped through the family room and stormed into the kitchen, ignoring Miley, who was right on his heels.

"I can't believe this!" he shouted.

"I'm not playing it," Mr. Stewart responded, thinking his son was annoyed at him for playing his video game. "I'm just making sure it's age appropriate, like a good parent should."

But Miley and Jackson ignored him. They had a bigger problem to deal with.

"Jackson, I'm sorry," Miley said.

"Sorry doesn't pay the bills, sister," Jackson said.

"No, that would be me," Mr. Stewart interjected, clearly puzzled by their argument. "Somebody tell me what's going on."

"I got fired," Jackson told his father. Shocked, Mr. Stewart hit the PAUSE button.

"Oh, no, Jackson. What did you do?"

he asked his son accusingly.

"I didn't do anything," Jackson said, defending himself. "You did."

"Me?" Mr. Stewart asked. Now he was *really* confused!

"Yeah, you had to have a second kid, and now Little Miss Big Mouth got me fired," Jackson said, pointing his thumb in the direction of his sister.

"Is that true, Mile?" Mr. Stewart asked.

"I was just trying to help," she told her father. "And besides, Jackson, I said I was sorry. What else do you want from me?"

"Oh, I don't know . . . a job?" Jackson suggested.

"I'm a kid!" Miley exclaimed. "How am I supposed to get you a job?" She paused and then added sarcastically, "Unless you want to be, like, Hannah Montana's assistant or something."

But Jackson didn't get the joke. "I'll take it," he said quickly.

"What?" Miley asked, trying to figure out what had just happened.

"The job. It's perfect," Jackson said.

"Uh-oh." Within seconds, Mr. Stewart had grasped just how much trouble this new plan could cause. He quickly returned to his video game.

"No, it's not," Miley said, backpedaling as quickly as she could. "I'm your little, big-mouthed sister. You don't want to be my assistant."

"You're right," Jackson admitted. "Assistant is demeaning. Let's go with senior vice president in charge of . . . 'assistication.' I'll start tomorrow at nine—wait, make it ten. I gotta get some business cards made."

Miley was trying to think of something, *anything*, to say in response to this, but it was too late. Jackson bounded upstairs to get started on his new career, and she was left in the living room, wondering how her world had just been turned upside down.

Then she heard a *splat* come from the video game and remembered that she had someone on her side, someone who could help her out of this jam. . . .

"What just happened?" she asked her father.

"I hit an armadillo, and Hannah got herself a new senior vice president of assistication," her father said with a chuckle.

"But I don't need an assisticant!" Miley protested.

"Well, you should've thought of that before you offered him the job," Mr. Stewart said.

"But this is a horrible idea," Miley said, pouting.

"Probably is. So I guess you better get up there and fire him," Mr. Stewart said.

"Dad, I can't!" Miley said. "I already cost him one job today. I can't fire him from another. That would be awful." She paused and looked at her father. Time to use a little sugar, she thought. "You do it," she suggested sweetly.

"Oh, no," Mr. Stewart said. "You made this mess, you gotta go up there and clean it up."

"But, Daddy, I—I can't," she whined.

"That's the deal, bud," he said decisively.

Miley knew that tone. There was no arguing with it. She started to climb the stairs, but she did so very, very slowly.

"Okay, okay, fine, I can do this," she said, trying to sound confident. "I'm gonna go up there and tell him—I can be strong. I'm gonna go up there and—"

No. She just couldn't do this, no matter how much of a pep talk she gave herself.

She stopped and said dramatically, "Daddy, please bail me out. Do I always have to learn something?"

"Honey, I'm just trying to teach you how to be a mature adult," he said reasonably. "Now, if you'll excuse me, I got a po-po roadblock in front of me and an army of evil turkeys on my tail." Mr. Stewart turned back to the game, which was making evil turkey gobbling sounds.

Chapter Three

Miley and Lilly were dressed as Lola and Hannah and ready to go to Hannah's CD signing. But they couldn't head out just yet, because they were waiting for Jackson.

"Jackson, come on, where's the limo? We're gonna be late for the CD signing!" Miley called to her brother-turned-assistant.

"Chillax," Jackson yelled back. "I'm on it right now, boss!"

Lilly couldn't get over this new arrangement. She knew no good could come of it.

"Wow," she said to Miley. "Jackson is your assistant. This is a horrible idea. A horrible, horrible idea. I'm talking your-dad's-old-mullet horrible."

"Lilly," Miley said, protesting.

"I know," Lilly said wearily. She had heard Miley's defense of her dad's mullet a million times before. "It was a different time. The chicks dug it."

"Lilly," Miley said again, "stop."

"Right. We were talking about you hiring Jackson. Horrible, horrible, horrible," Lilly declared.

"C'mon," Miley said. "I'm trying to give Jackson a chance. It's the least I can do. And I could use a little support here."

"You're right," Lilly admitted. "You're being a very good sister. And who knows, maybe he'll rise to the occasion."

Miley looked at her friend skeptically. "Do you really believe that?"

"Do you want support or the truth?" Lilly asked, exasperated. "Make up your mind."

Just then, Jackson came down the stairs wearing a nice suit and talking on his cell phone.

"This is absolutely unacceptable and I can tell you that Hannah Montana will never use your limo company again. Good day, sir . . . I said good day!" He slammed the phone shut.

"Jackson, what happened?" Miley asked, fearing the answer.

"They don't have a limo. And they're saying it's my fault because I didn't make a reservation. Can you believe that?"

"You know, I can," Lilly admitted.

"You didn't make a reservation?" Miley

cried. How hard was it to pick up the phone and book a limo?

"Miles, the company's called Ready When You Are Limos, not Ready When You Are Limos If You've Made a Reservation," Jackson said defensively. "I think it's pretty clear who's at fault here."

Lilly mouthed the word "horrible" to Miley, just in case her friend had forgotten what she thought of this whole idea. Miley, in turn, mouthed the words "zip it" to Lilly and turned back to her brother.

"Jackson, what am I gonna do now?"

"Look, it's not a problem," Jackson insisted. "I'll just drive you to the CD signing in my car. Sit in the back, close your eyes, it'll feel just like a limo."

The girls reluctantly agreed. After all, they didn't have much of a choice. Still, they sensed that this was *not* going to go well.

When they got to the record store, their appearance was a little more disheveled than they would have liked. Actually, it looked as if they had gone through a wind tunnel — and they might as well have, since Jackson had driven them to the signing with the convertible top down!

The store was packed with adoring fans eager to catch a glimpse of their favorite teen idol and get a CD signed. Jackson entered the store, with Miley and Lilly, both looking like little troll dolls, in tow.

"Again," he said to the girls, "really sorry about the whole convertible top thing."

Miley and Lilly tried to smile at the fans, but they knew how they must look to the crowd.

"Hi, everybody," Miley, as Hannah, said, without her usual exuberance.

Lilly touched her arm and whispered, "You have something in your teeth."

Miley swiped her finger across her teeth and inspected the results.

"Ewww, it's a fly," she groaned.

Lilly had only one thing to say to that: "Nasty."

Somehow, Miley managed to smooth down her hair and make it through the signing. It wasn't exactly a perfect first day on the job for Jackson, but Miley tried to put a positive spin on it. With a beginning like that, he could only get better, right?

A few days later, Lilly stopped by the Shack on her way to Miley's house. Rico and Carmen were practicing their routine. Lilly noticed that Rico kept stepping on poor Carmen's toes.

"*Aye!*" Carmen squealed.

But Rico—being Rico—wouldn't admit that he'd done anything wrong.

"Come on, *mamacita*. No pain, no gain," he said in the same overconfident tone he used with everyone.

Meanwhile, Lilly couldn't get over the scene at the snack bar. There was a crowd of girls, seemingly dizzy with excitement over . . . Oliver. He was expertly juggling water bottles and mixing beautiful tropical smoothies—at the same time! He finished by putting down the water bottles with a flourish and presenting the smoothies, complete with little umbrellas and dry-ice smoke, to his audience. Everyone broke into loud applause.

Oliver himself had been . . . *transformed*. Sporting a tropical shirt, a pukka bead necklace, and a bedhead hairstyle, he looked positively hip.

And, to top it all off, he was actually smooth-talking his smoothie-drinking admirers.

"Here you are, ladies. My newest concoction—the Smokin' Oken Smoothie. Cool enough for the hottest babes on the beach."

The girls accepted the drinks with broad smiles, but Lilly was not amused.

"Excuse me. Coming through. Knew him when he was a dork," she shouted as she pushed her way through the crowd.

"What's crack-a-lackin', Lil-lay?" Oliver said in his new laid-back lingo.

Lilly looked at him in disbelief. It was as if an alien had taken over his body! Where was her good friend? Who was this imposter?

"What is wrong with you?" Lilly asked him.

"Face it, Lilly," Oliver replied with an air of arrogance. "I found my thaaang. And I'm working it."

Lilly just rolled her eyes. "Well, work your way over to get me two bottles of water."

"One bi-zzle of wi-zzle for the Liz-zle," Oliver said, whereupon he began doing more juggling tricks with the water bottles. Lilly wasn't at all impressed—she just wanted her water.

"I'm going to bizzle *you* if you don't knock that off," she warned before she snatched the bottles out of Oliver's hands and stormed off.

"Don't be a playa hater, skater!" Oliver called after her.

A moment later, a water bottle came flying at him, and he quickly ducked under the counter. He popped back up and shouted to Lilly, "Ha! You mizzled."

On her way out of the Shack, Lilly passed Rico and Carmen, who were still practicing their moves. They danced with great drama, à la Fred Astaire and Ginger Rogers, on the steps leading up from the beach. It was a sight to behold—until they reached the top. With a tremendous flourish, Rico spun Carmen so hard she went flying over the stair rail. Lilly could hear the poor girl moaning from the beach.

"*Aye, papi,*" Carmen said with a groan.

Rico, ever the gentleman, responded true to form. "Stop whining, Carmen! Just pop your shoulder back in and let's rumba."

Lilly shook her head and hustled off to Miley's as fast as she could.

Chapter Four

Miley wasn't in a much better mood, though. She had been trying to call Jackson on her cell phone, but he wasn't picking up.

"C'mon, Jackson, answer your phone," she begged. Then she realized that she was hearing the ringing in stereo. "I can hear it ringing. Why can I hear it ringing?"

She followed the sound to the kitchen counter, where she found Jackson's phone.

"That's why," she said, annoyed. She

picked it up and put on her best country bumpkin voice, just as Jackson had a few days before. "Why, hello there. You've reached Jackson, Hannah Montana's assis-ticant. I can't do any assisticating right now 'cause I forgot my phone. Hyuk, hyuk, hyuk."

Lilly walked in, drinking her bottle of water, just as Miley angrily slammed Jackson's phone shut.

"Stupid Jackson!" Miley shouted.

"What'd he do now?" Lilly asked with no surprise whatsoever in her voice.

Miley picked up a dress to show Lilly. "He picked up Hannah's dry cleaning."

"What's wrong with that?" Lilly asked.

"Then he dropped it in the parking lot," Miley explained, turning the dress around so Lilly could see the giant tire mark that ran across it.

Once again, Lilly exclaimed, "Horrible!"

"Stop saying that," Miley demanded. "I have to perform at the American Teen Music Awards tonight, and all I can think about is Jackson getting me there late, or bringing the wrong wig, or clogging up the green room toilet and blaming it on the Dixie Chicks."

Lilly seemed to think the solution to Miley's problem was fairly obvious.

"Why don't you just fire him?" she asked.

"I know, I have to. And I will," Miley promised. "First thing tomorrow."

"Miley—" Lilly pushed.

"Fine. I'll do it the minute he walks in the door. I'm just gonna say 'Jackson, you're—'" Miley's rant was interrupted by none other than Jackson, who walked in carrying a box and a big bouquet of heart-shaped balloons.

"—carrying a balloon-heart bouquet," she finished quickly.

"Yeah," her brother said shyly. "I just wanted to say I know I screwed up a few times this week. And anybody else probably would've let me go, but you didn't. And that means a lot to me. Thanks." He handed his sister the box. When she opened it, she found a pair of pretty earrings inside.

"Jackson, you got me earrings," she said, beaming. Her expression turned to anguish as she looked at Lilly. "He got me earrings."

"I know," Lilly whispered. "They're beautiful."

"I know," Miley whispered back. Then, acknowledging Lilly's stance on this whole situation, she added, "It's horrible."

"And I don't care how many paychecks it takes me to pay them off, it's worth it just to know that you believe in me," Jackson said.

"Uh-huh," Miley said, without conviction. "I do. You betcha."

"Now, I'm gonna go double-check on that limo for tomorrow night's awards show," he said confidently.

"It's tonight," Miley reminded him.

"I'm all over it," Jackson assured her as he headed upstairs.

"How can I fire him after this?" Miley asked Lilly.

"Too bad you can't just give him some stupid job at the awards show, so when he screws up, it doesn't matter." Lilly didn't realize it, but her suggestion was the perfect solution.

"Come on, Lilly, that's just—brilliant!" Miley shouted.

"I know," Lilly said.

❊ ❊ ❊

Later that day, Miley had a rehearsal at the awards show venue.

"Hannah Montana rehearsal. Take one," the stage manager called out.

Dressed as Hannah, Miley went onstage to go over her "I Got Nerve" routine with Sean, one of her backup dancers. The theme was boxing, so the set included a boxing ring, a speed bag, and a heavy bag. As Miley and Sean practiced the choreography, Jackson waited off to the side, mimicking Sean's moves with gusto. When Miley finally finished, she headed offstage where Jackson had a towel ready for her.

"Great rehearsal, Sean," Miley said to the dancer.

"You, too, Hannah," Sean replied with a smile.

"Thanks," she said. "Take ten. You deserve it." As Sean walked away, she took the towel from her brother and joked, "So do I."

"Great job," Jackson said. "So what do you need me to do now, boss? Should I check the soundboard? Inspect the trapdoors? Make sure none of those big, heavy lights come crashing down during your number?"

"No, no, no," Miley said quickly. "Get away from the trapdoors and stay away from the lights and—stay away from everything. *Everything*," she repeated for emphasis.

Jackson looked at her helplessly. "Well, what am I supposed to do?" he asked.

"I've got a special job for you," she told him. "And it's the only thing I need you to do today. Nothing else. Just this. Everything else, once again, stay away."

"Bring it," Jackson challenged. He

clearly thought he was being given an important task.

"I want you to go to every single member of the crew and tell them how much I appreciate their hard work," Miley said dramatically.

Jackson looked at her as if he were awaiting further instructions. When it was clear nothing more was coming, he said, "That's it? That doesn't seem like a very important job."

"Oh, trust me, it's important," Miley assured him. "Goodwill makes for a good set, a good set makes for a good show. And a good show makes for a happy pop star," she finished, smiling a big, fat, fake smile.

Jackson looked confused, but he indulged his sister. "Okay . . ." He shrugged and headed off to start his job.

"And if you finish, go around again! And

again! And again! Spread the love!" Miley shouted desperately after him. Then she turned to find her father, disguised as a member of her entourage, standing next to her. He had observed the whole exchange.

"You know, sooner or later, you're gonna have to face the music and fire him," Mr. Stewart told his daughter.

"Not anymore, I found an easy fix for this," Miley said. "I found out a way to utilize Jackson to the best of his abilities."

"By giving him a job to do he can't screw up?" Mr. Stewart asked.

"Exactly," Miley said with a big nod. She was proud of herself for finding a way out of the mess she had caused.

They both watched as Jackson and Vernon, a very large crew member, exchanged a heartfelt hug. As Jackson's feet dangled above the floor, Vernon, with tears in eyes, said, "You tell Hannah Montana I love her, too."

Trying to find the breath to speak, Jackson replied, "Whatever you say . . . please put me down."

After speaking to everyone else he could find, Jackson finally made his way to Sean, Hannah's backup dancer. Sean worked a kink out of his neck as Jackson rambled on about how much Hannah appreciated all of his hard work.

"So keep up the good work and remember, Hannah loves you," Jackson said to wrap up the little speech he had now mastered. He held out his arms for a hug. Sean gave him a wary glance, but Jackson looked so pathetic that Sean finally gave in and offered Jackson a hug. A very brief, very awkward hug.

Even so, it wasn't brief enough. Sean's

neck pain flared up again and he cried out, "Ahh!"

"You want me to fix that for you?" Jackson asked enthusiastically.

Sean considered this. He *was* in a lot of pain. And he *did* have a big performance that night. . . .

"You can do that?" he asked.

"Oh, yeah. No problem," Jackson said casually, as if he actually had the qualifications to mess with a professional dancer's neck. He moved in behind Sean. "Just turn around, relax, and . . ." He lifted his knee to Sean's back and put on pressure until he heard a very loud *CRACK!*

"I didn't do it!" Jackson yelled, immediately jumping away.

"My back! What did you do?" Sean shouted.

Jackson was a wreck. "I don't know. It

worked when Scooby did it to Shaggy!" he said frantically.

"That's a cartoon!" Sean reminded him loudly.

"No, I was talking about my cousins," Jackson corrected him. "Just try and walk it off."

"I would . . . if I could walk," Sean said. He was in so much pain that he was having trouble talking. "Aw, man, I can't dance like this. I gotta go tell Hannah."

Jackson went a little crazy when he heard that. If Miley knew about his medical misstep, she would fire him for sure. The earrings were nice, but they weren't *that* nice.

"No, no, no!" Jackson protested. "What you can do is find someplace to go lie down. Out of sight. Where no one will find you."

"But Hannah said that—" Sean started

to explain. But Jackson interrupted him.

"Don't worry, I'll tell Hannah everything she needs to know," Jackson said.

"She should hear it from me. I mean, you said we're friends, right?" Sean said, referring to the little speech Jackson had just made.

Jackson thought quickly. How could he keep Sean from talking to Hannah? "No, you're not. She hates you."

"What?" Sean asked in disbelief.

"Yeah, yeah, yeah, the whole appreciation thing? My idea. You should probably just go. Put a little ice on it. And heat. Ice, then heat. Stretch," he advised. He just wanted Sean out of the way, so he could figure out how to fix this situation before Miley found out about it.

Sean limped off slowly, while Jackson walked off in the opposite direction, whistling nonchalantly as if everything were perfectly fine. As he passed several crew members, he said, "Hey, Hannah loves you," to one, and "Hannah loves you," to another. And then, "You're her favorite, sweeper guy," to yet another.

But as soon as he was alone, he took off at a run. He had to make this right, and he didn't have much time.

Chapter Five

"**A**nd now performing her new hit, 'I Got Nerve,' teen pop sensation, Hannah Montana!" As the announcer called her name, Miley was feeling confident. After all, she thought, everything is under control. She was glad that she had assigned Jackson such an easy task.

The crowd cheered as the music started and the lights came on, revealing Hannah Montana in a dazzling satin boxing robe.

She shared the stage with a hooded boxer, whom she assumed was Sean. He was shadowboxing with his back to her.

Miley launched into her song. As she sang the next line and danced across the stage, she grabbed the boxer and turned him around—only to discover that he wasn't Sean. He wasn't even *close* to being Sean. He was Jackson!

Miley's eyes widened with alarm.

Jackson mouthed, "I got it," as if that would reassure her. But this was Jackson—there was no reason to assume he had it *at all*!

In desperation, Miley turned back to the cameras and tried to go on with the song. She sang and danced her heart out, hoping to make up for whatever was going on behind her.

But every once in a while, she just had to

glance back at Jackson to see what he was doing. Each time he was in some terrible dancing predicament—getting tangled in the boxing-ring ropes or hitting himself in the face with the speed bag.

This was a nightmare! Jackson was trying to copy the moves he had seen Sean doing earlier, but he couldn't pull them off. After all, he was Jackson. What had he been thinking?

Miley kept on performing, hoping to get to the end of the song without a total disaster. And that might have worked—if Jackson hadn't finally lost his balance completely and crashed right into her. They landed in a tangle of arms and legs.

"Jackson!" Miley shouted as the song mercifully came to an end.

"I'm fired, aren't I?" Jackson asked.

"Ya think?" Miley asked, her voice sharp with anger and embarrassment.

They hurried offstage, and Miley stormed away. She wanted nothing to do with her brother for the rest of the night, at the very least. The way she felt right now, she wanted nothing to do with him for the rest of her *life*!

The next day, Mr. Stewart found Jackson on the couch, playing his video racing game. But he wasn't competing with his usual gusto. In fact, he wasn't even steering with his hands. He was using his chin instead.

When Mr. Stewart saw Jackson run over a chicken without even stopping, he knew something was really wrong.

"What's the matter, son? You didn't even try to miss that one-legged chicken. And he's just hopping in one place," Mr. Stewart said.

"Who cares?" Jackson said, sounding depressed. "I'll probably just mess it up like I messed up being Hannah's assisticant." He turned off the game just as Miley came down the stairs. She knew Jackson and her father hadn't seen her, so she paused to eavesdrop on their conversation.

"First of all," Mr. Stewart said, "'assisticant' ain't a word. And second, don't be down just because things didn't work out with you and your sister. It doesn't mean you're going to mess up everything. You did great down at Rico's," Mr. Stewart offered, trying to cheer his son up.

"I know, and I liked it, too," Jackson admitted.

"Maybe that's why you were good at it," his father suggested.

"Well, it doesn't matter anymore," Jackson said quietly. "I'll never get that job back." He got up and left through the front door. Miley quickly ducked back up the stairs, so Jackson wouldn't know she had been listening. The minute he was gone, though, she came back down to talk to her dad.

"I feel so bad. I opened my big mouth and got him fired, then opened it and got him hired, then fired. Maybe I should just keep my big mouth shut," Miley said regretfully.

"Oh, honey, let's face it . . . you'll never be able to keep that big mouth shut," Mr. Stewart pointed out.

Miley gave her father a pained look.

"I know!" she said miserably.

"It's okay, bud." Her dad draped his arm around her shoulders. "Just remember: next time before you say something, think it through."

"You're right," Miley agreed. But then a lightbulb seemed to go off in her head, and she added excitedly, "Wait a minute, I think I know how to fix this."

"Slow down, bud," he reminded her.

"Right again," Miley said. "Let me really think it through . . . before I open my big mouth this time."

She thought for exactly two seconds and said, "Yep, that'll work!" She started to walk out of the house before she realized her father wasn't with her. "Let's go! I know how to get Jackson his job back at Rico's."

"How are you going to do that?" he asked.

"Easy," Miley said with a smile. "I just gotta make a deal with the little devil."

It was the day of the big ballroom dance.

The deal Miley made with Rico involved her dressing up in a slinky red dress and standing in for Carmen, whose injury from her tumble onto the beach prevented her from dancing.

A spotlight hit Miley and Rico, and they began their tango. They danced beautifully, passing a rose back and forth between them for added showmanship.

Despite her misgivings about dancing with Rico, Miley was pleased with her performance. But at the end of the routine, Rico, known for his poor dipping skills, nearly dropped Miley.

In exasperation, she grabbed him, spun him around, and dipped him in one smooth motion, ending with a flourish.

"Now that's how you dip, ya' dip," she said proudly.

As Miley and Rico danced the day away,

Lilly and Oliver sat at the snack bar, watching Jackson behind the counter. There was no doubt about it; he just didn't have Oliver's finesse. As Jackson joyfully handed a pretty girl a drink, Oliver said bitterly, "Look at that. No style. No presentation. No flair. I can't believe I lost my job to him."

Together, he and Lilly watched Jackson try to impress another pretty girl who had approached the counter. He threw water bottles up in the air, trying to juggle them the way Oliver did. The difference was that Jackson's routine ended when one of the water bottles clocked him in the head, sending him to the floor. But he popped up quickly, giving the girl a two-finger point that he had copied from Oliver.

"That'll be three dollars . . . m'lady," Jackson said.

So, Miley was assisticant-free, Jackson was back to being only so-so at his job, and Oliver was back to being . . . Oliver. All was right with the universe again.

Put your hands together
for the next Hannah
Montana book . . .

Don't Bet on It

Adapted by Ann Lloyd

Based on the series created by Michael Poryes and Rich Correll & Barry O'Brien

Based on the episode, "Bad Moose Rising," Written by Steven James Meyer & Douglas Lieblein

For once, the house where Miley Stewart lived with her dad, Robby, and her brother, Jackson, was calm and quiet. Her dad was especially grateful for this today, because he was feeling seriously under the weather.

Even the birds chirping outside the window made his head throb.

But the peaceful atmosphere was too good to last, of course. It always is.

The silence was suddenly disrupted by pounding on the front door. Miley's dad, wearing a ratty old robe and blowing his nose, walked slowly down the stairs.

"As if I didn't feel bad enough already," he said with a moan as he saw who his visitor was.

Mr. Dontzig, the Stewarts' next-door neighbor, was standing in the doorway looking angry. Mr. Stewart reluctantly opened the door and let him in.

"Stewart! I'm sick of your leaves in my pool!" Mr. Dontzig bellowed as he waved a maple leaf in his neighbor's face.

"And I'm sick of your face in my house," Miley's dad said. Then he coughed and turned to collapse onto the couch. Being sick was exhausting.

Mr. Dontzig waved the leaf in the air, trying to fan Mr. Stewart's germs away from him, "Whoa, Jethro," he said, taking the opportunity to make fun of his neighbor's Southern background. "Since you're not whittling right now, try using your hands to cover your mouth."

Patty, Mr. Dontzig's eight-year-old niece, suddenly poked her head under her uncle's arm. She was wearing a swimsuit, nose clips, goggles, and a floatie.

"Uncle Albert, I wanna swim!" she whined. "What's taking so long? You said the hillbilly was scared of you."

Mr. Dontzig gave Mr. Stewart a cold, icy stare. "He is."

Over on the couch Miley's dad shivered. Then he sneezed and pulled his robe tighter around him. Being sick was not fun, and he was probably the worst patient on the planet. He shook again, feeling chills from his fever.

"See," Mr. Dontzig said to Patty as he imitated Robbie's shivering. "I've got him trembling."

Patty looked at Mr. Stewart and shrugged. "Come on," she said to her uncle. "I'm only here for the weekend. You said we'd do stuff."

But Mr. Dontzig couldn't take his eyes off Mr. Stewart. He knew his icy stare was making the guy tremble. "Stop nagging," he said to his niece.

"I wanna do stuff!" Patty said, stomping her foot.

"Stop nagging!" Mr. Dontzig yelled.

"I wanna do stuff!" Patty whined louder.

"Stop nagging!" Mr. Dontzig said, echoing

Patty's whine. He turned to Miley's dad. "I don't know where she gets it from." Then he remembered the reason he'd come over to the Stewarts' in the first place. He threw the large leaf on the ground. "Keep your leaves out of my pool!"

With that, Mr. Dontzig and Patty left.

Miley's dad sighed. Finally, he could get some peace and quiet. He put his achy head down on the couch.

"Dad?" Miley called. She was concerned—her dad was lying on the couch in his pajamas!

Mr. Stewart looked up to see Miley and Lilly standing over him. "It was nice while it lasted," he mumbled, rubbing his head.

"Dad, why aren't you dressed?" Miley asked. "The Stella Fabiana Fashion Show is tomorrow, and you promised you'd take me and Lilly to the mall to get shoes, make-up, and manicures."

"You did," Lilly added. "I remember. I was there."

Miley and Lilly were very excited about going to the fashion show. Miley had been invited because she was also singing super-star Hannah Montana. Lilly was going with her as Lola, Hannah's best friend. They were sure to see amazing new clothes and meet other celebrities—but they had to look just right for the event.

Miley tried to get her dad to move. "Come on, come on, let's boogie!"

Mr. Stewart sneezed and grabbed a tissue from his pocket.

"Not that kinda boogie," Lilly said, disgusted.

He blew his nose again, then looked at his daughter. "Sorry, honey I don't know if

I'm gonna be able to take you. This thing knocked me flatter than Uncle Earl's inflatable butt cushion after football season."

"Now there's a mental picture I really didn't need," Lilly commented.

"It's okay, Dad," Miley said, giving him a hug. "Feel better. Get well. I'll just make Jackson take us."

After all, thought Miley, what are big brothers for if not to drive their little sisters around town?

But Jackson had heard her from upstairs, and he had a very different opinion.

"Noooo!" Jackson screamed. He slammed his bedroom door and stomped down the stairs. "No, no, no, no, no, no!"

Miley watched her brother as he entered the room and stopped right in front of her.

"Not gonna happen—uh-uh—no way!" he ranted on. "Cooper and I are going to the Dodger game today. And I'm breakin' in a new foam finger." From behind his back, Jackson pulled out a large, blue foam finger.

"Jackson," Miley said. "Lilly and I have stuff we have to do, and you go to a baseball game practically every week."

"This is so unfair." Jackson complained to his dad. "Every time you can't haul her all over town, I'm the one who gets stuck doing it. I miss baseball games, basketball games, parties. I mean I have a life of my own and . . ." Jackson looked at his little sister. "I'm sick of you ruining it!"

Mr. Stewart's head was throbbing, and his kids' fighting was making him feel worse. He glared at Jackson. "And I'm sick as a dog. Stop complaining. Take your sister where she needs to go. I'll get you tickets to another game."

Jackson sighed. "Fine," he said as he headed for the front door. "Now what am I supposed to do with my new foam finger?" He looked sadly at his new blue finger . . . which wouldn't get to go to a game.

"Oh, I know, you can use it to wipe away your tiny, little tears," Miley said, wiping a pretend tear from her eye as she and Lilly followed him to the door. She made a boo-hoo face suitable for a three year old at Jackson. Then she quickly reverted to acting her actual age and gave her brother a stern look. "Get over it."

Being a teenager can be tricky.

DISNEY
Wizards
OF WAVERLY PLACE